THIS WALKER BOOK BELONGS TO:

_____

_____

_____

_____

red nose readers

One, Two, Flea!
Allan Ahlberg
Colin McNaughton

One, Two, Flea!
Tiny Tim

WALKER BOOKS
AND SUBSIDIARIES

LONDON • BOSTON • SYDNEY

First published 1986 by
Walker Books Limited
87 Vauxhall Walk
London SE11 5HJ

This edition published 1987
Reprinted 1989, 1994, 1995, 1997, 1999

Printed in Hong Kong

British Library Cataloguing in Publication Data
A catalogue record for this book is
available from the British Library.

ISBN 0-7445-1018-X

One, Two, Flea!

One, two, three,
mother finds a flea,
puts it in the teapot
to make a cup of tea.

The flea jumps out,
mother gives a shout,
in comes father
with his shirt hanging out.

Four, five, six,
father's in a fix,

wants to get the billy goat
to hatch a few chicks.

The chicks hatch out,
father gives a shout,

in comes granny
with her hair sticking out.

Seven, eight, nine,
granny's doing fine,
scrubs all the children
and pegs them on the line.

The line gives way,
granny shouts 'Hey!'
'Wow!' shout the children…

...and they all run away.

Tiny Tim

I have a little brother,
his name is Tiny Tim,
I put him in the bath-tub
to teach him how to swim.

He drinks up all the water,
he eats up all the soap,
he goes to bed
with a bubble in his throat.

In comes the doctor,
in comes the nurse,

in comes the lady
with the alligator purse.

'Dead!' says the doctor.
'Dead!' says the nurse.
'Dead!' says the lady
with the alligator purse.

But he isn't!

POP!

I have a little sister,
her name is Lorelei,
I push her up the chimney
to teach her how to fly.

She runs about the roof-tops,
she chases all the crows,
she goes to bed
with a feather up her nose.

In comes the doctor,
in comes the nurse,

in comes the lady
with the alligator purse.

'Dead!' says the doctor.
'Dead!' says the nurse.
'Dead!' says the lady
with the alligator purse.

But she isn't!

The End